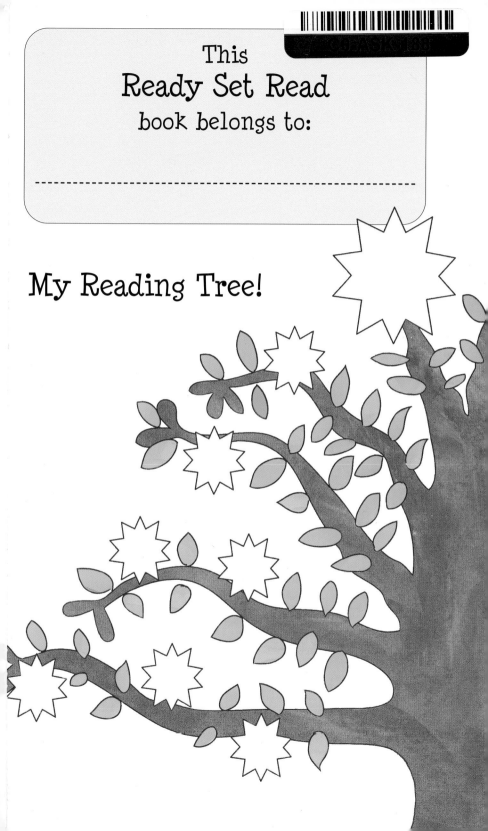

This
Ready Set Read
book belongs to:

My Reading Tree!

In memory of my dad ~ M. C.

For Lynn and Oberon ~ D. R.

LITTLE TIGER PRESS
An imprint of Magi Publications
1 The Coda Centre, 189 Munster Road, London SW6 6AW
www.littletigerpress.com

First published in Great Britain 2004
by Little Tiger Press, London
This edition published 2011
Text copyright © Michael Catchpool 2004
Illustrations copyright © David Roberts 2004

LTP/1800/0261/0611
ISBN 978-1-84895-368-0
2 4 6 8 10 9 7 5 3 1

Hopping Mad!

Michael Catchpool

illustrated by David Roberts

LITTLE TIGER PRESS

Fred lived next door to Finn.
Fred had five frogs, and so did Finn.

One night, when the moon was up and the grass was damp, Finn's five frogs called to Fred's frogs, "Come on over! We're having a party!"

"What an excellent idea!" Fred's frogs croaked back. "We'll be right over!" And they hopped over the fence.

The frogs dived and splashed and flipped
and flopped and had a fantastic time.
By the time the sun was coming up,
they could hardly hop.

"Phew!" croaked Fred's frogs.
"We really need to get home!"
And they dragged
themselves back over
the fence.

The next morning, as the sun sparkled on the water, Fred stood idly counting his frogs.

"One, two, three, FOUR!"

Then he looked over the fence
and counted the frogs in Finn's pond.
"One, two, three, four, five, SIX!"
Fred was furious.

9

"Frog thief!" he shouted at Finn.
"You should have five frogs, but you
have six. You've stolen one of mine!"
    Fred marched into Finn's
yard and snatched a frog
before Finn could say a word.

"This will stop you from stealing!" shouted Fred, and with some wood and some nails, he built his fence higher and higher.

That evening, as an owl swooped across the sky, Fred's five frogs called to Finn's five frogs, "Come over to our pond tonight for some fun."

"What an excellent idea!" croaked Finn's frogs.

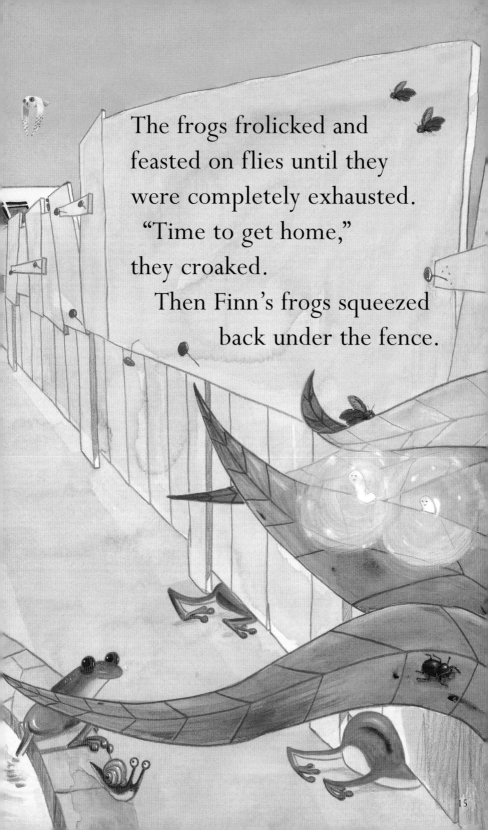

The frogs frolicked and
feasted on flies until they
were completely exhausted.
"Time to get home,"
they croaked.
Then Finn's frogs squeezed
back under the fence.

The next day, as the birds were singing in the trees, Finn slowly counted his frogs, "One, two, THREE!"

He glared over the fence into Fred's pond. "One, two, three, four, five, six, SEVEN!"

Finn was fuming. "Frog thief!" he shouted at Fred. "You have seven frogs, and I've only got three."

He marched right around to Fred's yard and snatched back his two frogs.

"I'll stop you from taking my frogs!"
said Finn, and he dug a big, wide ditch.

That evening, Finn's five frogs called
to Fred's frogs, "Want to party in our
pond tonight?"

So Fred's frogs scrambled over the huge
fence and leaped over the enormous ditch.

The frogs had a splendid time, diving and swimming, dancing and singing until they could barely croak.

Just before dawn, Fred's frogs returned home. They leaped back over the enormous ditch and scrambled back over the huge fence.

The following morning,
while the dew glistened on
the grass, Fred carefully
counted his frogs.
"One, TWO!"

Then he counted the
frogs in Finn's pond.
  "One, two, three, four,
five, six, seven, EIGHT!"
  Fred was frantic.

"Frog thief!" he shouted at Finn. "You've stolen three of my frogs!" He marched through the gate and snatched back his frogs. "I'll put a stop to this," Fred said, and he put a great big cage right over his frogs and his pond.

That evening, Fred's five frogs called to
Finn's frogs, "We can't play tonight.
We've been locked up."

"Then we'll come over to you," croaked
Finn's frogs, and they leaped across the great
big ditch, over the high fence and opened the
door of the cage.

"Phew!" said Fred's frogs. "You know,
we frogs need our freedom." And they
hopped off, with Finn's frogs
close behind.

Now Fred has no frogs.
And neither does Finn.

But Fiona, who lives four doors down, has TEN!

Croak! Croak! Croak!

Super Search!

Look at the picture below. Put the word stickers next to the correct objects in the picture. We've done one for you.

★ When you have put all the words in the right places, add the first star to your reading tree!

✩ Picture Dictionary

Look at the words below. They are all types of insects.
Put the correct picture sticker next to each word.

beetle   dragonfly

moth   bee

Have you got these right? Then put a star on your reading tree!

✩ Sentence Order

All stories are made up of **sentences**. Tick the sentence
below that came **last** in the story.

- [ ] But Fiona, who lives four doors down, has TEN!
- [ ] Now Fred has no frogs.
- [ ] And neither does Finn.

★ Did you get this right?
Remember to add another star to your reading tree!

True or False

Fred tried different things to stop Finn from stealing his frogs. Which of these sentences are true and which are false?

	True	False
1) He built his fence higher.		
2) He built a brick wall around the pond.		
3) He put a great big cage right over his frogs and his pond.		

★ Did you get this right? Add another star to your reading tree.

Crazy Commas

A **comma** is a mark that is used to separate words. A comma sometimes tells the reader where to pause in a sentence.

E.g. The next morning, as the sun sparkled on the water, Fred stood idly counting his frogs.

Put a comma into each sentence below.

1) Fred had five frogs and so did Finn.
2) Just before dawn Fred's frogs returned home.
3) And they hopped off with Finn's frogs close behind.

★ Did you get these right?
Then add another star to your reading tree!

Time to Rhyme!

Words that have the same sounds as one another are called **rhyming words**. E.g. back – tack. The words below all rhyme with words from the story! Put each word sticker next to the word it rhymes with.

1) dig _____

2) floor _____

3) dog _____

4) towel _____

5) date _____

6) sun _____

★ Did you get these right?
Remember to add a star to your reading tree.

Perfect Plurals

A **noun** is a naming word – a person, place, or thing.
A **plural noun** shows there is more than one person, place, or thing. An **s** at the end of a noun often means that it is plural.

E.g. one cat – two cats

Circle the plural nouns in the sentences below.

1) Fred used some nails.

2) You have seven frogs, and I've only got three.

3) Fiona lives four doors down.

4) The birds were singing in the trees.

Did you find these plural nouns in the story?

★ Did you get these right?
Then add the last star to your reading tree!